DISCA

for Martha Ullman West

The Man Who Played Accordion Music

by Tobi Tobias / Illustrated by Nola Langner

ALFRED A. KNOPF / Publisher / NEW YORK

This is a Borzoi Book published by Alfred A. Knopf, Inc.   Text Copyright ©1979 by Tobi Tobias. Illustrations Copyright ©1979 by Nola Langner. All rights reserved under International and Pan-American Copyright Conventions. Published in the United States by Alfred A. Knopf, Inc., New York, and simultaneously in Canada by Random House of Canada Limited, Toronto. Distributed by Random House, Inc., New York. Manufactured in the United States of America. 10 9 8 7 6 5 4 3 2 1

wheezing music came swinging and zinging through the walls.

The housewife, squeezing oranges for freshly squeezed orange juice, fishing out the pits and the rough bits of pulp, so that her family would be happy, stopped what she was doing to listen.

It was the man next door. That Hungarian man. The accordion player. Nobody knew anything about him.

But you can know because you are not in the story and because I trust you.

His name was Anton Zoltany. He was fifty-six years old. He had a black mustache. His dark eyes said anything and everything. He came from a family of trapeze artists, the famous Flying Zoltanys, but Anton Zoltany was born with a crippled leg and couldn't fly through the air. His only gift was music.

Nobody knew anything

Where did he work? What did he do? How did he live? Nobody knew. Some people said he was secretly very rich. Others said he was poor but very happy. Some said he was crazy. But nobody really knew.

about him because he lived behind his closed apartment house door.

The only thing they knew was the wild, happy music he sent through the walls, the notes swimming out from the keys and buttons and the slow opening and closing fan of his accordion, the melody dancing out from

Zoltany's heart.

This morning the music sang to the housewife, especially to her, a song with her name on it.

"Man, what are you doing," the housewife cried out, "making this singing, this secret singing, in my heart?"

But there was no answer. Just the sound of the cascading music getting faster and faster every minute.

"Leave your work," Zoltany's music whispered.

"Let it go," it called a little louder.

"Sing and dance", it cried out,

twisting and whirling. "Out the door."

And the housewife forgot the cooking and the cleaning and the sorting and ordering. She thought of rainbows. She forgot the shopping and washing and coming and going. She thought of ships sailing, sailing. She forgot her husband and children and house and cat. She was thinking of a world she had always imagined where, instead of doing what her family needed, she would do as she pleased.

"*Meow*, where's my breakfast?" said the cat, coming as close to growling as a tiger-striped tomcat can.

"Get it yourself,

Silly old cat", said the housewife, and went laughing and dancing out the door.

Her husband, George McGeorge, the children's father, the head of the household, came into the kitchen and found no freshly squeezed orange juice and no wife. George McGeorge was a sharp and tidy, up-to-the-minute, up-to-date person because he worked with computers. The unexpected was not what he expected. Here it was a brilliant Monday morning, the beginning of the workday week. George McGeorge was ready to eat a hot, nourishing, handmade breakfast and unfold the news of the day from his crackling newspaper. Then he would call his two children—a beautiful set of twins—downstairs and see that they were bright and shining, neat and smart, ready for school. After that he would go to his office with the closed glass windows, run things through his computers, and get the results.

But there was no breakfast, no wife. The kitchen was empty, except for the cat. There was only the music, seeping softly through the walls, strumming into the sink and the clock and the stove.

complained the cat, sulking over his dish.

"Don't you think I know that?" said George McGeorge, upset. "She gives *me* freshly squeezed orange juice, hot oatmeal cooked slowly for twenty-five minutes, eggs any way I ask and always perfect. She gives me hot coffee made from freshly ground coffee beans."

"With cream," the cat reminded him.

"With cream," said George McGeorge sadly.

"And what do you give her?"

the music whispered slyly. But this father of twins was not the sort of person who heard questions in music. He barely heard the tune. To George McGeorge the music was only noise, and too much noise at that.

"Crazy Hungarian," he muttered, absent-mindedly munching on a handful of Friskies.

Just then the children, Sam who was six, and Samantha who was six and a minute, beautiful twins, alike as each other, came down the stairs with their shoelaces and their homework undone.

"Your mother seems to have stepped out," their father said.

"That's all right," said Sam.

"She always comes back," said Samantha.

"We can make our own breakfast," said Sam, sloshing water over a column of frozen orange juice.

"Sure," said Samantha, flipping two frozen waffles into the toaster.

Zoltany's accordion jiggled out a little tune about skipping and sliding and running away. To Sam and Samantha it sounded like holiday music. But it put a terrible, uneasy feeling inside George McGeorge. It made him feel he should put everything in order and nail it down tight, so that it wouldn't get loose and disappear.

The music floated through the walls, growing happier and happier.

It made Sam think of jelly beans.

It made Samantha think of Christmas.

"Have you brushed your teeth and your hair?" asked their father.

The music grew faster and faster.

It made Sam think of riding a bicycle downhill.

It made Samantha think of staying up late.

"Have you made your beds and cleaned your room?" their father cried.

The music grew louder and louder.

"Have you practiced the piano?"

It made Samantha think of merry-go-rounds.

It made Sam think of laughing until his stomach hurt, and Chinatown, and getting dirty.

"Do you have your permission notes? Are you wearing socks that match?"

"What?" yelled Sam and Samantha.

"It's time to get everything in order," George McGeorge shouted back. "We have duties and responsibilities. I must get ready for work and you must get ready for school."

"Oh no," said Sam.

"Today is a holiday," said Samantha.

"Socks?"

"We are going to the zoo," they said together.

"To the zoo, to the zoo," they sang to Zoltany's tune.

The music danced so fast it flew.
The children swooped and whirled with
it, grabbing their sweaters with the
missing buttons and dashing out the
door. Their feet rattled down the six
flights of metal fire stairs like a bag of
spilled marbles. They went zooming
through the lobby, running pell-mell to
the street corner where there was a red
bus marked ZOO to take them exactly
where they wanted to go, non-stop.

Zoltany's accordion played a lovely, slow Hungarian song that meant "they will come back, safe and happy; they will come back, when they're ready," but George McGeorge didn't understand it. He never understood what music was telling him; he only knew what he saw. He stood in his empty kitchen and stared at the cat, and at the open front door beyond it that the twins, in their hurry, had forgotten to shut.

The music went on, slowly changing its tune.

"Stupid Hungarian, can't even play right," muttered George McGeorge. He might not be able to understand music, but he could sure enough tell wrong notes when he heard them, and these twangings and zangings were driving him wild. Poor George McGeorge. Half his mind was fixed on this never-stopping, queer-sounding music climbing all over his kitchen while the other half was trying to figure out what to do to put his life and his family, his home and his Monday, in neat and sensible order.

The notes that sounded like wrong notes to George McGeorge crept through the baseboards where the Zoltany wall and the Zoltany floor met the McGeorge wall and the McGeorge floor, just at the level—about eight inches off the ground—of the McGeorge cat.

They stalked around his sharp, furry, pricked-up ears and his moist, velvety, twitching nose.

They might be wrong notes to a computer man but, to a tiger-striped tomcat, they came out of the baseboards like gorgeous smells, reminding him, deep down in his tiger-striped heart,
of the things he liked best:

Fish! Love! Adventure!

"Twang," went Zoltany's music. It was the luscious, tangy, nose-filling smell of mackerel. "Swang," whined the accordion—the special, sweet, secret smells of love. "Zing-zong"—the fresh-air smells of adventure that make cats want to leap and bound and pounce through the air for nothing, roll wriggling on the soft-carpeted ground, paws waving at imagined balls of paper on a dancing string, as if they'd gone catnip crazy.

At the sound of Zoltany's music, the cat ruffled out his thick, glossy, orange-zigzagged coat. He gathered his muscles tight-together as if he were about to pounce on a sneaky, squeaky mouse. Looking his proudest, he swiveled his head, turned his huge, shining, yellow eyes on his master, meowed, "See you later, McGeorge," and bounded in one magnificent bound, out the open front door, landing surely and elegantly, as always, on his feet.

McGeorge ran after him, but he was too late. Cat, twins, wife were gone. McGeorge was furious. He strode to the next apartment door and pounded on the name *Zoltany* where it was printed under the doorbell.

The door was opened by a short man with a crippled leg and a black mustache. He had dark eyes that said anything and everything. The man was holding an accordion. The accordion was silent.

"Yes?" the man said.

"I want the music to stop," George McGeorge said.

Zoltany looked confused.

"I said I want that music to stop," said George McGeorge. "Can't you understand English?"

You and I know Anton Zoltany, though, and *we* know that he understands English, Hungarian,

and, most of all, MUSIC.

"Music cannot stop," said Zoltan, politely. "If you stop it in one place, it goes to another. Faster and louder, maybe. It breaks out, you see."

"This music must stop," George McGeorge demanded. "It does terrible things. It came through your walls and into my apartment. And look what's happened. My wife has skipped away from her housework and the children have run away from their homework. They've all dashed away from their duties and rushed away from their responsibilities. Even my cat is gone. My beautiful, bright, workday Monday is not the way I've planned it to be."

"Maybe," said the man with the accordion, "that's just as well." And politely, but firmly, shut his door. You might even say he shut it in George McGeorge's face, but it wasn't really that way because Anton Zoltany was an extremely polite Hungarian man.

One two three four five six seven eight nine seconds went by. George McGeorge stood there, outside the closed apartment house door. In absolute silence. And then the accordion music started up again,

singing to all the foolish hearts that

were ready to be set free.

TOBI TOBIAS is the author of over a dozen books for children, among them *Moving Day, The Quitting Deal,* and *Petey.* A well-known dance critic, Ms. Tobias is an associate editor of *Dance Magazine* and a contributor to television's *Dance in America* and *Live from Lincoln Center* series. She and her family live in the brownstone they have renovated on New York's Upper West Side.

NOLA LANGNER, who began her career as an illustrator in a television studio, has created the pictures for more than thirty books for children, including the award-winning *Scram Kid!,* and has both written and illustrated several more. Ms. Langner lives in New York City with her husband, their five children, and a number of Siamese cats.

Library of Congress Cataloging in Publication Data   Tobias, Tobi. The man who played accordion music. SUMMARY: A Hungarian man's accordion music disrupts the daily routine of the McGeorge family in the apartment next door. [1. Accordion — Fiction. 2. Apartment houses — Fiction] I. Langner, Nola.   II. Title. PZ7.T56Man   1979 [E]   78-11757 ISBN 0-394-83663-4 ISBN 0-394-93663-9 lib. bdg.

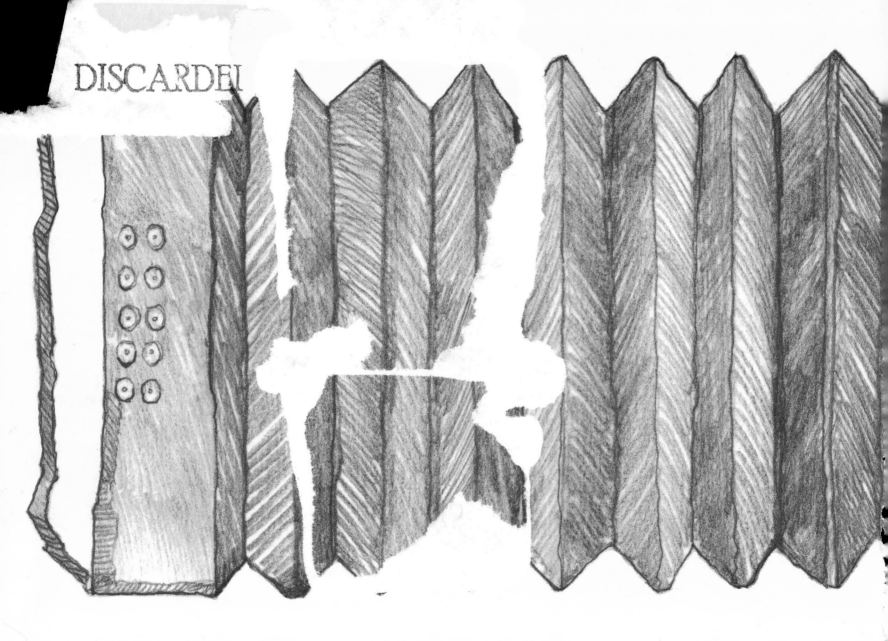